RACE CAR Count

Henry Holt and Company, LLC, *Publishers since 1866*
175 Fifth Avenue, New York, New York 10010
mackids.com

Henry Holt® is a registered trademark of Henry Holt and Company, LLC.
Text copyright © 2015 by Rebecca Kai Dotlich
Illustrations copyright © 2015 by Michael Slack
All rights reserved.

First Edition—2015 / Designed by April Ward
The illustrations for this book were digitally painted and collaged in Adobe Photoshop.

Printed in China by RR Donnelley Asia Printing Solutions Ltd.,
Dongguan City, Guangdong Province

10 9 8 7 6 5 4 3 2 1

Henry Holt books may be purchased for business or promotional use. For information
on bulk purchases, please contact the Macmillan Corporate and Premium Sales Department
at (800) 221-7945 x5442 or by e-mail at specialmarkets@macmillan.com.

Library of Congress Cataloging-in-Publication Data
Dotlich, Rebecca Kai.
Race car count / Rebecca Kai Dotlich ; illustrated by Michael Slack. — First edition.
pages   cm
Summary: "Count to ten with fast and colorful race cars" —Provided by publisher.
ISBN 978-1-62779-009-3 (hardback)
[1. Stories in rhyme. 2. Automobiles, Racing—Fiction. 3. Counting.]
I. Slack, Michael H., 1969– illustrator. II. Title.
PZ8.3.D7415Rac 2015   [E]—dc23   2014042958

For Wyatt
and Luke,
my little racers
—R. K. D.

To Iggy, Lily, and Stephanie,
Team Slebbs pit crew
—M. S.

RACE CAR COUNT

by **Rebecca Kai Dotlich**

illustrated by **Michael Slack**

Christy Ottaviano Books

HENRY HOLT AND COMPANY • NEW YORK

RED LIGHT,
YELLOW LIGHT,
GREEN LIGHT,
GO!

Race car **1** honks, *Look at me!*
He zooms in front with the turn of a key.

Race car **2**, all sleek and new,
blares—*Hey, look out, I'm coming too!*

Race car 3 flies through the rain.

A roar of blue zips down the lane.

Race car **4**, all shiny red,
rumbles, grumbles, pulls ahead.

Race car **5** is but a blink.

Her nickname—***BEEP!***—is Little Pink.

Race car **6** is going strong.
Steady does it, can't go wrong.

Race car **7** squeals, *I'm the best.*

His speedy engine aced the test!

Race car **8** is dynamite—
thunders, roars, swerves to the right.

Race car 9 goes blowing by.
SHOW-OFF! She's not camera shy.

Race car 10 has finished last.
Still, his wheels were lightning fast.

All lined up, **10** in a row . . .

RED LIGHT,

YELLOW LIGHT,

GREEN
LIGHT ...

MEET THE RACE CARS!

Race car 1

NAME:
Lucky

LOVES:
spinach

COLLECTS:
old fenders

Race car 2

NAME:
Duke

LOVES:
cheesy pizza

COLLECTS:
goggles

Race car 3

NAME:
Tumbly

LOVES:
snow cones

COLLECTS:
tools

Race car 4

NAME:
Scoot

LOVES:
spicy meatballs

COLLECTS:
radiators

Race car 5

NAME:
Small Fry

LOVES:
bubble gum

COLLECTS:
keys

Race car 6

NAME:
Derby

LOVES:
mac & cheese

COLLECTS:
oil caps

Race car 7

NAME:
Chaser

LOVES:
blueberry pancakes

COLLECTS:
nuts & bolts

Race car 8

NAME:
Sparky

LOVES:
hot peppers

COLLECTS:
spark plugs

Race car 9

NAME:
Comet

LOVES:
milk shakes

COLLECTS:
hubcaps

Race car 10

NAME:
Groovy

LOVES:
popcorn

COLLECTS:
bumper stickers